Look for the **Scooby-Doo Mysteries**.
Collect them all!

Written by
James Gelsey

A
LITTLE APPLE
PAPERBACK

SCHOLASTIC INC.

New York Toronto London Auckland Sydney
Mexico City New Delhi Hong Kong

For Mom and Dad

ISBN 0-590-81914-3

19 18 17 16 15 14 13   · 2 3 4 5 6/0

Special thanks to Duendes Del Sur for cover and interior illustrations.

Printed in the U.S.A.

First Scholastic printing, January 1999

"Hey, Scooby, you're fogging up the windshield," Fred said. "It's hard enough to see with all this snow."

The Mystery Machine was heading up the only road on Big Pine Mountain. Scooby was sitting on the front seat, wedged between Velma and Daphne.

Velma wiped the windshield with her hand and peered through the opening. "It looks like it's been snowing for quite a while."

Daphne smiled. "We sure picked a good weekend to go skiing," she said.

1

"I'll bet the trails will be great," Fred added.

Suddenly, Fred saw something on the road and slammed on the brakes. Right in front of the van was a big, hairy creature. It raised its arms and roared at the gang. Then the creature turned and ran into the woods.

"Is everyone okay?" Fred asked.

"Zoinks! What was that?" Shaggy asked from the backseat.

"I'm not sure," Fred answered.

"It looked like a person," Daphne said.

"Or a bear," Velma said.

"Or, like, maybe a hungry skier looking for a snack shop," Shaggy offered.

"Well, whatever it was, it's gone now," Fred said. "I say we get moving to the lodge."

"Good idea, Fred," Daphne said. "I don't like the idea of getting stuck in this snowstorm."

"Velma, how much farther?" Fred asked.

Velma was being scrunched by Scooby-Doo. She didn't even have enough room to unfold the road map.

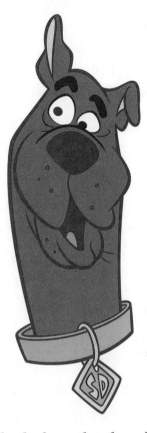

"You know, Scooby," Velma said, "this seat wasn't meant for three people and a Scooby-sized dog."

"There's plenty of room in the back with Shaggy," Daphne said.

"Ruh-uh!" Scooby said, shaking his head.

"Would you go in the back for a Scooby Snack?" Velma asked.

"Rope," Scooby barked.

"Two Scooby Snacks?" Daphne asked.

"Ruh-uh," Scooby replied.

"Three?" Fred said.

"Rorget it." Scooby continued to stare out the fogged-up windshield. Every so often, he'd wipe the glass with his big pink tongue to clear it off.

"All right, Scooby-Doo, what's with you?" Fred asked.

Shaggy poked his head up front. "Like, he's just mad at me 'cause I called him a scaredy-cat," he said.

"Why'd you do that?" Daphne asked.

"Because he told me he would rather stay in the lodge than ski," Shaggy replied.

"Shaggy, there's nothing wrong with that," Velma said. "Many people prefer to stay in the lodge. They can sit by a warm fire, bundle up under a nice wool blanket, and sip hot cocoa."

Shaggy's ears perked up. "Did you say, like, hot cocoa?"

Velma nodded.

"Scoob, old pal," Shaggy said, "if sitting in the lodge and drinking hot chocolate makes you a scaredy-cat, then I only have one thing to say."

"What's that?" Daphne asked.

"Meow," Shaggy answered.

Everyone laughed as Scooby hopped into the back with Shaggy.

With Scooby gone, Velma finally had room to check the road map.

"The lodge is just a few miles up," she reported. "We should be there any minute."

"Well, gang," Fred said, "our ski weekend is about to begin."

"With lots of hot cocoa," Shaggy said.

"And lots of peace and quiet," Daphne added.

Chapter 2

It was still snowing as the Mystery Machine pulled up in front of Big Pine Lodge. The gang piled out and headed in through the front door.

Inside the lodge, there was a huge fireplace with a few sofas and large chairs around it. There was a ladder in front of the fireplace. A giant moose head sat at the top.

Scooby looked up at the moose head. "Rikes!" he barked, jumping behind Shaggy.

"Easy, pal," Shaggy said. "That's just an old stuffed moose head. There's nothing to be afraid of. It's not alive."

Suddenly, the moose spoke.

"Welcome to Big Pine Lodge," it said.

"Zoinks!" Shaggy exclaimed, jumping behind Fred. "It's alive!"

An old man appeared from behind the moose head on the ladder. He picked up the moose head and hung it over the fireplace. Then he climbed down the ladder.

"Just having a little fun," he said. "Welcome to Big Pine Lodge. I'm Terence Squall."

Daphne held out her hand. "Hello, Mr. Squall," she said. "I'm Daphne Blake. We spoke last week."

"Of course, Daphne," Terence said. "My, you're almost as pretty as my granddaughter. But don't tell her I said that."

"Said what?" came a voice from behind Terence.

"Oh, nothing," Terence said, blushing.

 "I'm Cindy Squall," the young woman said. "I'm Terence's granddaughter. Welcome."

Terence walked over to the fireplace. "Where's that boyfriend of yours with that wood?" Terence asked. "He's been gone nearly an hour now."

"He'll be back," Cindy said.

Terence leaned toward the fire and poked at some of the logs. "For someone who hates the cold, it sure takes him a long time to go between the house and the wood shack," Terence muttered.

There was a loud rapping on the back door. Cindy walked over and opened it. In walked a big man carrying an armload of firewood. He stamped his feet twice to get the snow off his boots.

"About time," Terence said under his breath. "Over here, Cam," he called. "This fire's about to die. These poor guests will freeze to death if we don't get some fresh logs on the fire."

The man with the armful of wood slowly walked to the fireplace and dropped the wood on the floor with a loud crash.

"Avalanche!" Shaggy screamed, jumping into Scooby's arms.

"No, just firewood," Cam said. He took off his parka but kept his red scarf wrapped around his neck. "I'm Cam Filbert, Cindy's boyfriend. If you need anything, just ask Cindy or Terence." He turned and headed over to the front desk.

"How about a snowplow?" said a voice coming down the stairs. "The name's Ruckus, L. Richard Ruckus," he said. He was wearing a gold national ski team jacket. "The radio in my room says the road up the mountain is closed. Seems that the snowstorm set off a small avalanche."

"Like, wow," Shaggy said.

"That means there's no coming or going," Terence said. "Probably won't be cleared for at least a day."

Cam frowned. "If we lived down south," he said, "we could be outside right now, playing tennis in shorts and T-shirts."

Cindy reached up and gave Cam's scarf a playful tug.

"Oh, Cam," she said. "You know I can't leave Big Pine Mountain as long as my grandfather runs the lodge."

"But I've got a lead on a great place down south," Cam replied.

Terence handed the gang the keys to their rooms. "Even if there wasn't a snow-storm," he complained, "no one would be here anyway. As long as that snow monster keeps hanging around, I'll be ruined for sure."

"Snow monster?" Shaggy and Scooby said together.

Fred, Daphne, and Velma all looked at one another.

"What snow monster?" Fred asked.

Cindy walked behind the counter and put her hand on her grandfather's shoulder. "There's no snow monster," she said. "It's probably just that old man who lives in the woods."

"You mean Shakey McGraw?" Terence asked. "I don't know about that." He shook his head and walked over to the large couch.

"I do know that if this snow monster stays around, I won't be able to keep the lodge open."

Mr. Ruckus sat down next to Terence on the couch. "As I told you before, Mr. Squall," Mr. Ruckus said, "I'm looking for a very private place to practice my skiing. It will take more than some snow monster to scare me away from these ski trails."

All of a sudden, a grumbling sound filled the room. Everyone looked scared.

"It's the snow monster!" Mr. Ruckus yelled. "It's here!"

Shaggy and Scooby started laughing.

"What's so funny, you two?" Velma asked.

"Like, that wasn't any snow monster," Shaggy said. "That was Scooby's stomach."

"Rot cocoa time," Scooby barked.

Cindy smiled and turned to Scooby. "Okay, Scooby," she said. "I'll get you some hot cocoa. But only because I know you'll protect us from the snow monster if it really does show up." Cindy walked over to Scooby and scratched behind his ear.

Scooby sat up and looked as brave as he could.

"Rou bet!" he barked.

Chapter 3

The guests of Big Pine Lodge sat inside and waited for the blizzard to stop. The snow was piling up and the sky was very gray.

Daphne stood by the window and finally said, "Hey, everybody, it stopped snowing!"

Mr. Ruckus looked up from waxing his skis. "Finally," he said. "Now we can see how good these ski trails really are."

"Only if it's safe," Velma added. Everyone looked over at Cindy, who was standing behind the front desk.

"The trails should be great," she said. "It's time to hit the slopes!"

"Like, don't you mean it's time to hit the kitchen?" Shaggy asked. "All this waiting has made me hungry."

Cindy smiled at Shaggy. "Why don't you make at least one run down the mountain?" she asked. "You're not a scaredy-cat, are you?"

"Not me," Shaggy said, shaking his head. Shaggy jumped out of the chair, grabbed some ski poles, and pretended to ski. "Whoosh! Whoosh!" he said.

Mr. Ruckus ran over to Shaggy and grabbed the poles.

"These are not toys," he said. "These are the most expensive ski poles that money can buy." Mr. Ruckus turned away and carefully examined the poles for damage.

Cindy put on her parka. "Shaggy, there's a ski shack at the top of the mountain. It's got lots of skis and other equipment you can borrow. Everyone ready?"

Fred, Daphne, Velma, Shaggy, and Mr. Ruckus all nodded. Scooby remained curled up by the fire.

"What about you, Scooby?" Cindy asked. "Aren't you coming?"

Scooby sat up and shook his head.

"Ruh-uh," he said.

"But you'll love it up on the mountain," Cindy said. "I'll tell you what. You can ride up the mountain with me. What do you say?" Cindy looked right into Scooby's eyes and smiled.

Scooby couldn't resist Cindy's sweet smile. "Rokay," he said, jumping up.

"Watch out for the snow monster," Terence said with a smile.

"Whatever," Mr. Ruckus said, walking past Terence. "I've got to get a good ski run in today." He pushed through the gang and walked out the back door.

"Just forget about Mr. Ruckus," Fred said. "We're here to have a good time."

Everyone followed Cindy out the back door and along a path. They walked past a big white barn and a small wooden shack. Just as they were heading into the woods, they heard a man's voice coming from one of the trees.

"Gee-ronimo!" the man called. He came crashing down on Scooby-Doo. "Gotcha now, you big old snow monster!"

"Relp! Raggy!" Scooby called. Everyone rushed over and pulled an old man with a long beard off Scooby.

"Shakey McGraw!" Cindy exclaimed. "What are you doing?"

"I'm catching me a snow monster," he replied. "Ooooh, my back."

"Like, that's no snow monster," Shaggy said. "That's Scooby-Doo."

Shakey squinted his eyes and looked at Scooby.

"Thought you were the snow monster," he said. "It's around here, you know."

"You saw the snow monster?" Velma asked.

"Plain as the nose on my face," Shakey answered. "Saw it come out of the wood shack. It tried to get me, but I was too fast. It'll eat you right up if it catches you, you know."

"Shakey, you've got to stop scaring people with these snow monster stories," Cindy said. "And you owe Scooby an apology."

Shakey turned to Scooby and said, "Sorry about that. No hard feelings." Shakey winced in pain and grabbed his back. "Gotta stop jumping out of trees," he said. "Have a good ski day, folks." Shakey turned and limped away, disappearing into the woods.

"What a strange man," Daphne said.

"He is a little strange," Cindy agreed. She turned and continued on her way. The gang followed her along the narrow path winding through some tall pine trees. It ended right by the ski lift.

"Jinkies, I guess people didn't make it up here before the blizzard," Velma said. Most of the chairs on the ski lift going up the mountain were empty.

"It's so beautiful," Daphne gasped. "It looks like someone threw a giant white blanket over the whole mountain."

"Or spilled some marshmallow fluff," Shaggy joked. He and Scooby laughed. "Just imagine, Scoob." They stopped laughing as they slipped into a daydream of sliding down the mountain, licking up the marshmallow fluff as they went.

"Come on, you two," Fred called, snapping Shaggy and Scooby out of their daydream. "Hop in a chair." Fred and Daphne were already seated and headed up the mountain.

"Come on, Shaggy," Velma said, "you ride with me." The two of them

21

were scooped up into a chair and went on their way.

Cindy turned to Scooby. "Stand here, Scooby," she instructed. "When the chair comes behind you, just sit back." Before Scooby knew what happened, the chair swept them up. Off they went, swinging up the mountain. Scooby looked over the side of the chair and saw the ground fall away.

"Rikes!" he said, clutching the seat with all four paws.

"Don't worry, Scooby," Cindy assured him. "It's a short ride, and you'll be perfectly safe on top of the mountain."

Chapter 4

Velma and Shaggy were waiting at the top of the mountain when Scooby-Doo and Cindy arrived.

"Where are the others?" Cindy asked.

Velma pointed a few yards away. They saw Mr. Ruckus zip up his jacket and head down the experts' ski slope. As he skied away, his red scarf flapped in the wind. Daphne and Fred were getting ready to go down a different trail. They adjusted their goggles and hats and then skied off.

Cindy turned to Velma and Shaggy. "Now then, let's see what the ski shack has

23

for you." Cindy reached for two pairs of skis and handed them to Velma and Shaggy.

"These should be about right," she said.

"Cindy, how are you and Scooby going to get down?" Velma asked.

Cindy thought for a minute and turned to Scooby. He was busy digging in the snow.

"Scooby, would you like to ride down the mountain with me?" she asked.

"Rokay!" Scooby said with a big smile.

"Great, we'll ride on my snowboard," Cindy said.

"Ro way!" Scooby barked with a big frown.

"Come on, Scooby, you'll love it," Cindy said.

"It's like surfing on snow," Shaggy said.

"Ruh-uh," Scooby said. He refused to budge.

"Wait right here," Cindy said. She walked over to the ski shack and returned with a green and orange snowboard. She put it down by Scooby's feet.

24

"Like, I don't think anything will get Scooby to go down the mountain on that thing," Shaggy said.

Then, from behind the ski shack came a loud growl.

"Grrrrrrrrrrrroar!"

"Except maybe a snow monster!" Shaggy yelled.

"That's no snow monster," Cindy said. "That's just Shakey McGraw playing a joke on us." Cindy folded her arms and stood with her back to the ski shack. "Shakey, we know it's you, so just come on out."

But Shakey didn't come out from behind the shack — the snow monster did! It had blue fur all over its body and big white teeth. The creature raised its arms and let out another roar.

"Just ignore him and he'll stop," Cindy said.

"But it is the snow monster!" Velma exclaimed.

"Very funny, Velma," Cindy said.

The snow monster walked toward them, growling the whole way. Velma, Shaggy, and

Scooby stepped away, and Scooby heard something go *click*. He looked down and saw his feet strapped onto the snowboard. He couldn't get out.

"Cindy, look out!" Velma called. But it was too late. The snow monster grabbed Cindy and held her tight.

"Shakey, what are you doing?" Cindy yelled. The monster picked her up and threw her over its shoulder.

The monster roared at Velma, Shaggy, and Scooby.

"We have to get help," Velma said. She turned and started skiing down the mountain.

"So, like, let's get out of here," Shaggy said.

"Raggy!" Scooby called.

"Like, I hate to do this, buddy," Shaggy said. "But you'll thank me later when you haven't been eaten by the snow monster."

Shaggy gave Scooby a slight push, and then started down the slope himself.

Scooby was snowboarding down the mountain — and he was out of control!

Chapter 5

ack down the mountain, Fred and Daphne were sitting in a big sleigh behind the lodge. Terence placed a pile of green wool blankets and some thermoses inside the sleigh.

"You're going to love this sleigh ride," Terence said. "You keep an eye out for Cindy and your friends. I'm going to the barn to get the horses." Terence turned and headed over to the barn.

"Look out below!" Velma's voice suddenly filled the air. She came whizzing down a narrow path and skied into a big snowdrift by the sleigh.

"Scooby-Dooby-Doo!" Scooby yelled as he snowboarded right into the snowdrift behind Velma.

"Zoinks!" Shaggy shouted as he skied into the snowdrift right behind Scooby.

Fred and Daphne jumped out of the sleigh and ran over to the snowdrift. Daphne helped Velma up. Scooby crawled out of the snowdrift and shook the snow off himself.

"You shoulda seen it, man," Shaggy said, standing up. "It was enormous."

Scooby stood up on his back legs and stretched as high as he could.

"It was roaring like a lion with razor-sharp teeth," Shaggy continued.

"Rooooar," Scooby said, trying to imitate the snow monster.

"What are you talking about?" Fred asked.

"Velma, are you okay?" Daphne asked.

Velma cleaned her glasses and straightened her jacket. "Yes, I'm fine," she said. "And it *is* real."

"What is?" Fred and Daphne asked.

"The snow monster," Velma replied. "And it got Cindy!"

Just then, Cindy came skiing down the same path. She came to an easy stop just next to the sleigh.

"Rindy!" Scooby called, his tail wagging. He ran over and gave her a lick.

"But I thought the snow monster got you," Shaggy said.

"You don't live on a mountain without knowing how to protect yourself," Cindy said. "I managed to break free, and I hopped on these skis. Someone, it seems, borrowed my snowboard." She looked at Scooby. Scooby grinned and blushed a little.

Terence suddenly screamed from the barn. The horses whinnied, and the barn door flew open. The snow monster came roaring out of the barn. It growled at everyone and headed straight for them.

"Oh, no!" Shaggy cried. "It's back!"

Shaggy and Scooby jumped into the sleigh and hid under the blankets. Fred, Daphne, Velma, and Cindy tried to back away, but the monster was fast. It reached over and grabbed Cindy. Cindy tried to break free, but the monster held her tight. It threw her over its shoulder and then ran roaring off into the woods.

"Was that what you saw on the mountain, Velma?" Fred asked.

"Yes, that was it," she answered.

"It looks familiar," Daphne said.

"You're right, Daphne," Fred said. "That must have been what we almost hit on the road driving up here."

"This snow monster really knows its way around the mountain," Velma said. "Almost as if it knows where we are at all times."

"I think there's something funny going on here," Fred agreed. "It's time to look around."

A big slurping sound came from under the blankets in the sleigh. Fred threw off the blankets and found Shaggy and Scooby sipping hot cocoa from the thermoses.

"Like, it's cold out here," Shaggy said. "There's no point letting it go to waste."

"All right, you two," Daphne said, "it's time to get to work. Cindy's been kidnapped for real this time."

"And we have to help find her," Velma said.

"Right," Fred said. "Daphne and I will follow the monster's trail into the woods. You three go over to the barn to check on Terence."

"Why was Terence in the barn?" Velma asked.

"He was getting the horses for the sleigh," Daphne replied. "That's when we heard his scream."

"Right," Fred agreed. "See what you can find. We'll meet back in the lodge in half an hour."

Chapter 6

Shaggy, Scooby, and Velma walked over to the barn. Inside, they saw the horses in their stalls but no sign of Terence.

"Mr. Squall?" called Velma.

"Like, nobody here but us horses," Shaggy said.

"That's very odd," Velma said as she looked around. "Hey, look at this." She pointed to the floor. "There are two sets of footprints. One is Terence's, and the other must belong to the snow monster. Let's see where it leads."

They followed the footprints out the

barn's back door. The tracks led to a small shack behind the barn. Inside were some stacks of firewood. And hanging on a hook right by the door was a red scarf.

"Jinkies," Velma said. "What a clue! What do you think about this, Shaggy? Shaggy? Scooby?" Velma turned, but Shaggy and Scooby weren't there. She walked outside and saw them playing in the snow next to the shack.

"Oh, brother," Velma said. "Shaggy, Scooby, I'm going back to the lodge to meet Fred and Daphne." She turned and headed down the path to the lodge.

"We'll be right behind you, Velma," Shaggy called. "Just as soon as we finish our snowman."

Scooby grabbed a pawful of snow and started rolling it into a snowball. Scooby kept rolling and rolling until the ball was almost as big as he was.

"Scooby-Doo, I'm going to go to the wood shack for some twigs for the snowman's body," Shaggy said. "I'll be right back." Shaggy walked over to the wood shack and opened the door. There was the snow monster!

Shaggy slammed the door shut.

Before Shaggy could run away, the wood

shack door burst open. The snow monster roared at the top of its lungs.

"Run, Scooby-Doo! It's the snow monster!" Shaggy yelled as he ran toward Scooby. The snow monster started chasing Shaggy through the snow.

"This way, Scooby," Shaggy said. The two of them ran and made a sharp left turn into an open field. They hadn't run more than three steps when Shaggy realized they had stepped onto a frozen pond.

"Whoooooooooooa!" they called, sliding and spinning across the ice. The snow monster followed them onto the frozen pond and was gliding right behind them. Shaggy and Scooby were headed straight for a tree at the edge of the pond. As they neared it, Shaggy and Scooby put out their right arms and swung themselves clear around the tree and back onto the ice.

"Whoooooooooooa!" they called, gliding past the snow monster. The snow monster

watched Shaggy and Scooby slide by and didn't see the tree until it was too late. *BAM!* The snow monster hit the tree so hard that all of the snow on the branches came tumbling down right on top of him.

Shaggy and Scooby reached the other side of the pond and got off the ice. "Quick, let's get back to the lodge before it can get up," Shaggy said. They stood up and ran back to the lodge, leaving the snow monster under a pile of snow.

Chapter 7

Shaggy and Scooby ran down the path, around the lodge, and in through the front door. Once inside, they closed the door behind them.

"Quick, Scooby, give me a paw," Shaggy said. They reached over and dragged a big coatrack in front of the door.

"Hey, what are you two doing?" Daphne asked. She was standing by the front desk with Velma and Fred.

"Like, just blocking the door so no snow monsters can get in," Shaggy replied.

"I don't think you have to worry about

any snow monster," Fred said.

"Why not?" Shaggy asked.

"Because of some clues that we found," Velma said.

"Daphne and I found this caught on a branch in the woods," Fred said. He held out a piece of red cloth. One side of it had a row of fringe.

"Looks like a piece of a red blanket," Shaggy said.

"Or a piece of a red scarf," Velma said.

"Like the one in the shack!" Shaggy exclaimed.

"Or the one Mr. Ruckus was wearing," Fred added.

"Or the one that Cam wears all the time," Daphne said.

Velma turned and walked over to the back door.

"Come check this out," she called. The gang walked over and saw a small pile of snow and ice inside the back door. A couple of huge, wet footprints headed toward the desk.

"This pile of melted snow tells me that someone recently came in the back door with snow on his feet," Velma said.

"But where do the footprints lead?" Daphne asked.

"They could lead anywhere," Velma said.

RAP, RAP, RAP. Everyone jumped at the rapping that came from the back door. Fred opened the door and Mr. Ruckus limped into the room. His ski jacket was torn in two places and he had a scratch on his hand. He used a piece of a branch as a cane. As he closed the door, Cam squeezed in behind him. He was carrying an armload of firewood. He stamped his feet twice before continuing over to the fireplace.

"I tried the front door, but it was locked," Mr. Ruckus said.

"What happened to you, Mr. Ruckus?" Daphne asked.

"Nothing, really," Mr. Ruckus replied. He started for the stairs.

"The guy took a tumble on the experts' slope," Cam said, putting the firewood down.

Mr. Ruckus glared at Cam. "I did not take a tumble. I was all alone on the slope when someone — or something — ran right across the trail in front of me. Some reckless hot-dogger dressed all in blue. He startled me. I lost my balance and hit a rock. I think I twisted my ankle. But I did not take a tumble."

"Whatever you say, guy," Cam said. He took off his jacket and went into the office behind the front desk.

"If you don't mind," Mr. Ruckus said, slowly limping upstairs, "I'm going up to my room to rest."

Once Mr. Ruckus disappeared upstairs, Fred turned to the gang.

"Did anybody else notice that?" he asked.

"Yeah," Shaggy said. "He had a twig stuck in his hair."

"Not that," Fred said.

"Neither Mr. Ruckus nor Cam were wearing their red scarves," Daphne said.

"I have a hunch that this snow monster is a little hot under the collar," Velma said.

"And there's only one way to find out," Fred said. "Gang, it's time to set a trap."

Chapter 8

"**H**ere's the plan," Fred began. "We'll set the trap out back by the barn. We've had two sightings of the monster there already."

"Fred's right," Velma agreed. "There must be something there that the monster wants to keep people away from."

"Shaggy and Scooby," Fred continued, "you two have the easy part."

"Like, I've heard that before, Scooby," Shaggy said.

"All you have to do is play in the snow . . ." Fred began to explain.

"Rat's it?" Scooby asked with surprise. "Rokay!"

". . . until the snow monster shows up," Fred finished.

"Rorget it!" Scooby sat down and crossed his paws.

"Count me out, too," Shaggy said. "I'm not going to sit around in the snow just for some snow monster to come and eat me up."

"Come on, you two," Daphne said, "we need your help to catch the monster."

"Ro way!" Scooby said.

"And rescue Cindy," Fred added.

Scooby's ears twitched at the sound of Cindy's name. Scooby remembered how nice she was to him before.

"Will you do it for a Scooby Snack?" Velma asked.

"Rou bet!" Scooby said. Velma tossed Scooby a snack and he gobbled it down. "Yum!" he said, patting his belly.

"So, like, what's going to happen while Scooby and I are playing?" Shaggy asked.

"Velma, Daphne, and I will be hiding in the sleigh," Fred answered. "When the monster appears, we'll throw a sleigh blanket on him."

The gang went outside. Fred, Daphne, and Velma climbed into the sleigh and hid. Shaggy and Scooby started building another snowman. Shaggy rolled a big ball of snow for the body. Scooby rolled a ball of snow for the head and started shaping it.

"Hey," Shaggy said, "that doesn't look like a snowman. What is it?"

"Rowdog!" Scooby barked happily.

Then everyone heard the sound of someone running through the woods behind them.

"It's the snow monster!" Shaggy called. "Get ready, Freddy!"

Before they knew what was happening, someone ran out of the woods right at Shaggy and Scooby.

"Now!" Fred yelled from the sleigh. Fred, Daphne, and Velma stood up, holding a blanket. Fred took it in his hands and jumped from the sleigh, tackling the running creature under the sleigh blanket.

"Help!" yelled a voice from under the blanket. Terence suddenly burst out from the woods.

"Where'd you go, Shakey McGraw?" he called. "And where's my granddaughter?"

Just as Daphne and Velma were getting out of the sleigh, they heard a voice from above. It was Mr. Ruckus leaning out of his window.

"Do you people mind?" he called down. "How do you expect me to get any rest with all this shouting outside and some woman yelling inside here?"

"A woman yelling inside?" Terence asked. "It must be Cindy!" He got up and headed for the lodge. Velma and Daphne followed.

"Help! Help!" the voice cried from under the blanket.

Fred unwrapped the blanket.

"It's Shakey McGraw!" Shaggy exclaimed.

"If he's not the snow monster," Fred said, "then it must still be out there. But where?"

"Relp!" yelled Scooby. The snow monster appeared from the bushes, and it was holding Scooby's tail!

Scooby, trying to run away, kicked snow up into the monster's face. The monster let go and Scooby took off up the path. The snow monster cleaned off its face and ran after Scooby-Doo.

Chapter 9

Scooby ran along the path until he reached the ski lift. He saw the snow monster getting closer and jumped on the ski lift. The snow monster got on a few chairs behind Scooby.

At the top of the mountain, Scooby jumped off the ski lift and ran over to the ski shack. The snow monster followed. Scooby tried to hide behind the rack of skis, but the snow monster reached out and knocked the rack over. The skis and snowboards went everywhere. The snow monster got closer and closer to Scooby. As Scooby backed away, he kept tripping on the skis. He took two more steps and then he couldn't move. He looked down and saw his feet stuck in a snowboard.

"Ruh-roh," Scooby said.

The snow monster let out an enormous roar and reached over for Scooby. Just as it did, Scooby pushed himself away from the monster. The snowboard slid along the snow for a few feet and then started sliding downhill.

"Rot again!" Scooby said to himself. As Scooby picked up speed, he managed to turn around and face downhill. He was sailing down the mountain with the snow monster close behind.

Suddenly, the snow monster swerved in front of Scooby. The monster bumped into Scooby and they started rolling down the mountain. As they rolled, they gathered more and more snow until they became a giant snowball.

The snowball rolled all the way to the bottom of the mountain. Fred, Daphne, and Velma were waiting there, along with Terence and Cindy.

"Scooby-Doo, where are you?" Shaggy yelled.

"Rin here!" Scooby said. A moment later he poked his head through the snow.

Just then Shaggy came running up with a mountain ranger.

"Now that's what I call a snowdog," Shaggy said, laughing.

Terence and the mountain ranger pulled the snow monster out of the snowball. Terence reached over and yanked off the monster's mask.

"Cam!" Cindy cried.

"I was sure it was Shakey," Terence said.

"That's what we thought at first, too," Velma said. "But Shakey hurt his back jumping from the tree. There was no way he could carry Cindy away, much less pick her up twice."

"We also thought Mr. Ruckus was involved," Fred said. "He didn't make any secret about wanting a private place to practice for the national ski team."

"But once we saw him with his twisted ankle," Daphne continued, "we realized that he couldn't have been everywhere the snow monster was in such a short amount of time."

"We first suspected Cam because of the red scarf we found in the wood shack,"

Velma said.

"But what really tipped us off was when Cam told us how Mr. Ruckus hurt himself before Mr. Ruckus did," Fred said.

"The only way he could have known that Mr. Ruckus fell on the slope was if he was there," Velma added.

"And according to Mr. Ruckus," Daphne said, "there was no one around except for him and the snow monster."

Cindy looked at Cam. "How could you do this?"

Cam looked down at the ground. "All I wanted to do was scare Terence enough so that he'd sell this place and you'd come with me down south where we could be married. I was only doing this for us."

"No, you were only doing this for you," Cindy said. "There is no us anymore."

The mountain ranger took Cam by the arm and walked away.

Terence turned to Shakey. "I guess I owe you an apology," he said, extending his hand. Shakey looked at Terence's hand and then shook it.

"It's okay," Shakey said. "It's the most anyone's cared about me in years. Say, you wouldn't happen to have any hot cocoa, would ya?"

Terence smiled. "Sure, what do you say, Cindy? Cindy?" Cindy was gone. And, for that matter, so was Scooby-Doo.

"Over here," Cindy called. Everyone turned and saw Scooby and Cindy sitting in the sleigh.

"There's plenty of hot cocoa for every-one," she said. "But the first batch goes to the bravest dog around for capturing the snow monster." Cindy gave Scooby a kiss on the cheek.

"Scooby-Dooby-Doo!" Scooby cheered.

About the Author

As a boy, James Gelsey used to run home from school to watch the Scooby-Doo cartoons on television (only after finishing his homework). Today, he still enjoys watching them with his wife and daughter. He also has a real dog named Scooby who loves nothing more than a good Scooby Snack!

Solve a Mystery With Scooby-Doo!

SCOOBY DOO! MYSTERIES

by James Gelsey

Read them all!

Zoinks!

Ruh-roh!

$3.99 each!

#1: SCOOBY-DOO AND THE HAUNTED CASTLE
#2: SCOOBY-DOO AND THE MUMMY'S CURSE
#3: SCOOBY-DOO AND THE SNOW MONSTER

At bookstores everywhere!

SCO898